Daydreaming Digit Art

¡Haloween coloring book: Die of fear painting!

Daydreaming Digit Art

Haloween coloring book

We love receiving feedback from our customers.
If you can rate this colouring book on Amazon,
we will appreciate it, as it helps us to continue growing.

Made in the USA
Las Vegas, NV
30 September 2023